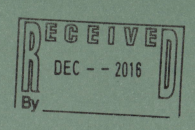

THE LONELY GIANT

In memory of my mum, Jane,
and for my family:
Jon, Henry, and Millie

Library of Congress Catalog Card Number 2015935059. ISBN 978-0-7636-8225-5.
This book was typeset in ITC Cheltenham. The illustrations were done in acrylic, watercolor, and colored pencil.
Candlewick Press, 99 Dover Street, Somerville, Massachusetts 02144. visit us at www.candlewick.com
Printed in Humen, Dongguan, China. 16 17 18 19 20 21 APS 10 9 8 7 6 5 4 3 2 1

THE LONELY GIANT

SOPHIE AMBROSE

CANDLEWICK PRESS

In a cave, on top of a crag, in the middle
of a huge forest, lived a giant. The giant spent
all day, day after day, doing what giants do . . .

pulling up trees as though they were weeds,

heaving and hurling huge logs like spears,

and smashing
and mashing
mountains.

Over the years,

smaller and

and quieter and

all the birds and the animals were scared away

the forest became

smaller

quieter until

and the songs of the forest had gone.

At night, the giant sat alone in his cold cave.
"How quiet everything is," he said with a sigh.
"I remember the forest being full of birdsong,
with plenty of wood for my fire."

The giant grew lonelier and lonelier.

Then one day, when the giant was hard at work bashing and smashing, a little yellow bird appeared.

She followed the giant all day long,
singing to him.

The giant enjoyed the little yellow bird's singing so much that he caught her and put her in a cage.

"Now you can sing to me whenever I want," he said. "I won't be lonely anymore."

But the little yellow bird grew sad,

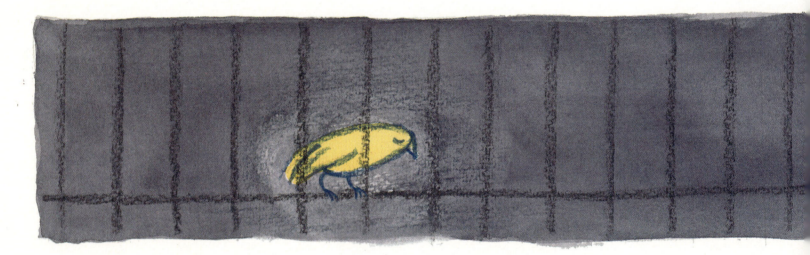

and the sadder she got, the less she sang.

Soon she was too sad to sing at all.

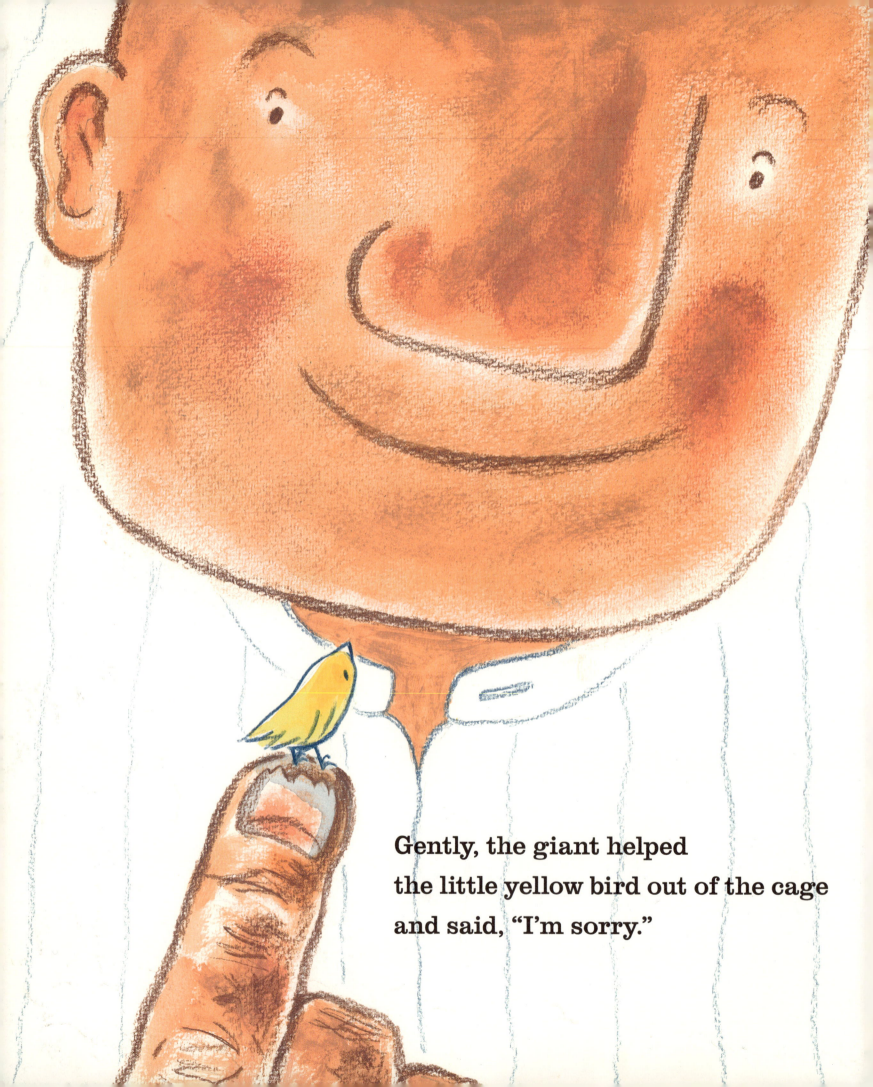

Gently, the giant helped
the little yellow bird out of the cage
and said, "I'm sorry."

The next morning,
when the giant looked
for the little yellow bird,
she had gone.

That day, the giant walked and walked, looking for
the little yellow bird. But there were no birds—
or trees or plants—to be seen.

"If only I could bring them all back," he said.
"I must fix what I've broken."

The giant worked hard to rebuild the forest.

He sowed seeds,

he mended mountains,

and he planted trees.

Then the giant watched and waited.

Slowly, over the years,

bigger and

and noisier and

all the birds and the animals came back

the forest became

bigger

noisier until

to their beautiful green home.

And the forest
blossomed with life again!

The giant wasn't lonely anymore.
He was happy at last.

And so was the little yellow bird,
whose song filled the forest all day,
every day.